340561

P3-4

This book is to be returned on or before
the last date stamped below.

READING COLLECTION

F
ARE

Falkirk Council

illustrated by
David Cox

D1461093

RISING ★ STARS

First published in Great Britain by
RISING STARS UK LTD 2004
76 Farnaby Road, Bromley, BR1 4BH

Reprinted 2004

For information visit our website at:
www.risingstars-uk.com

British Library Cataloguing in Publication Data

A CIP record for this book is available from the British Library.

ISBN: 1-904591-71-X

First published in 2003 by
MACMILLAN EDUCATION AUSTRALIA PTY LTD
627 Chapel Street, South Yarra, Australia 3141

Associated companies and representatives throughout the world.

Project Management by Limelight Press Pty Ltd
Cover and text design by Lore Foye
Illustrations by David Cox

Printed and bound in Great Britain by
Mackays of Chatham plc, Chatham, Kent

BOYS RULE!
Contents

Josh   *Con*

CHAPTER 1

Tent Tactics

Con has invited his best friend Josh
to sleep over at his house. They
decide to experience the thrill of
camping in the great outdoors by
spending the entire night in a tent—
pitched in Con's garden.

Josh "What if your garden was the Serengeti plains in Africa, we probably wouldn't make it through the night."

Con "Why?"

Josh "Because we'd be eaten alive by lions. They'd rip through this tent in a second and tear us to bits. They'd go for our necks, then our guts—sucking out all the blood and air."

Con "Sick!"

Josh "They do a lot of their hunting at night—I saw it on TV once. There was this scene where they attacked all these sleeping elephants—it was so cool."

Con "Not for the elephants. Besides, if we were really camping in Africa we wouldn't pitch our tent where lions hang out."

4

Josh "Yeah, I know. I'm just saying, that's all."

Con "Phwoh!! Did you just take off your socks?"

Josh (laughing) "Yes, well I did walk all the way over here after my game of basketball."

Con "We're in a tent! Maybe you could put your feet outside. Only joking!"

The boys chuckle and spend the next few minutes telling each other jokes. Eventually they decide to get some sleep. A few moments later, Josh jumps up out of his sleeping bag and flicks on his torch.

Josh "Did you hear that? Are you awake?"

Con (groggy) "What? Hmm? Yeah, now I am! What's up?"

Josh "I heard something."

Con "What? Lions?"

Josh "No, I'm not joking! It sounded like someone stepping on a stick."

Con "We don't have any sticks in my garden. Maybe you were dreaming it."

Josh "No, it was real. Something or someone's out there!"

Con "No they're not! Get back to sleep."

Josh reluctantly flicks off the torch. But it isn't long before he springs up again out of his sleeping bag. This time, he sees that Con is also sitting upright.

Josh "*Now* did you hear that?"

Con "Yeah, I did!"

Josh "It could be an escaped prisoner who's looking for a hide-out."

Con "Yeah, right—in my garden. Maybe I should have a look?"

Josh "No!"

Con "Why?"

Josh "Because if it is a prisoner he won't want to get caught and he might do something terrible to you. He could be really dangerous!"

Con "The only thing that's
dangerous are your smelly feet—
man, they're off! I'm nearly
choking in here."

Josh "Sorry—What can I do?"

Once again, the boys suddenly hear the sound of sticks snapping— they both jump with fright.

Josh "Oh no, he's coming to get us!"

Con "Shhh! Stop freaking out. You're scaring me."

Josh (whispering) "Sorry. But if it's not an escaped prisoner, what do you think it is?"

Con "I don't know."

Josh "Could be an alien?"

Con "You watch too much TV!"

Josh "Well it could be! Aliens come
down to Earth and take people all
the time. Especially if you're out in
the open like we are. They can
probably see us right now from
their spaceship."

Con "You mean they can probably *smell* us!!"

Suddenly a shadow appears from out of nowhere, standing at the entrance of the tent.

The boys scream.

"AAAAARRRRRRGHHHHHH!!!!!!!!!!"

CHAPTER 2

Phew!

It's only Con's dad. He tells the boys
to go to sleep because he can hear
them from inside the house. He
leaves them and goes back to bed.

Josh "Phew! Lucky it was just your old man."

Con "Aliens and escaped prisoners—huh! You crack me up!"

Josh "Well, you were scared, too—admit it."

Con "Yeah, but not as much as you."

Josh "I'm hungry."

Con "Yeah so am I—there's some cake in the fridge."

Josh "Yeah!"

Con "Let's go—but be quiet. I don't want to wake anyone up."

The boys leave the tent and tiptoe across the damp grass over to the back door of Con's house.

Con "Oh no! Dad's locked us out."

Con and Josh quietly wander around the house trying every door.

Con "I can't believe this. We're totally locked out. We'll have to climb through a window. Look, my sister's window is open. Shhhh! Be really quiet. We can't wake her up or we'll be in big trouble."

Josh (whispering) "This is so cool. I feel like some secret commando breaking in to catch some bad guys."

Con "You really *do* watch too much TV!"

The boys climb really quietly in through Con's sister's bedroom window and carefully sneak across the room. Just then, Josh's smelly feet connect with something—a loud, thunderous bang suddenly wakes up Con's sister. She screams as she sees the shadows of Con and Josh standing in front of her.

CHAPTER 3

Mystery Sound

Con's father and mother rush into
the room. They are not impressed to
see Con and Josh—even though the
boys try to explain how they were
hungry and locked out. After getting
a lecture and something to eat, Con
and Josh go back out to the tent.

Con "I think your big smelly feet are
a menace! First you stink out the
tent, then you wake everyone up!"
Josh "Sorry."

Con "Doesn't matter. I'm going to
sleep now. Goodnight."
Josh "G'night."

A few minutes later, directly
outside the boys' tent, there is a
sudden sound of sticks snapping—
again! The boys jump up out of their
sleeping bags and flick the torch on.

Josh "Is that your dad again? Please tell me it's your dad!"

Con "I don't think so."

Josh "See! I was right, the aliens are back."

Con "Well whatever it is—I'm going to look."

Josh "I'm coming with you!"

The boys unzip the tent and nervously stick their heads outside. They shine their torch frantically across the garden, but nothing is there. Suddenly, the stick snapping sound starts up again.

Both boys gasp! They direct the
torch up into the trees at the edge of
the garden, to discover the mystery of
the creepy sounds—a cat happily
chewing and scratching on some
branches.

Josh "A cat! That's it? A harmless cat!"

Con (chuckling) "I don't know about harmless. Maybe it's an alien cat or a cat that's escaped from a special cat prison or ..."

Josh "Yeah, yeah, really funny."

The boys pop their heads back
inside the tent and finally get to
sleep. The only sounds heard for the
rest of the evening are crickets
chirping, sticks snapping and ... oh
yes, some serious snoring!

BOYS RULE!

Camping Lingo

Josh

Con

air bed A mattress that you blow up with a pump. An air bed is really comfortable to sleep on.

compass A compass shows you where north, south, east and west are.

cool box You put your food in a cool box to keep it fresh. It's a good idea to take a cool box when you go camping.

torch A torch is a light you can carry. It's really important to take a torch with you when you go camping.

33

BOYS RULE!
Camping Must-dos

☞ Make sure you don't pitch your tent near an animal burrow.

☞ Don't forget to take the insect repellent.

☞ Take plenty of food.

☞ Make sure that you put your campfire out before you go to sleep.

☞ Tell ghost stories before you go to sleep—it might scare away the creepy-crawlies!

☞ Make sure that your friend doesn't snore.

☞ If you camp in the garden, make sure your parents don't lock the door. You might want to go inside in the middle of the night.

☞ If you are camping out near a river, make sure you don't sleepwalk—you might get wet!

☞ If you have a dog, let him sleep in the tent with you. Dogs are good at scaring wild animals away.

☞ The most important thing to remember to take camping is toilet paper, and a spade to bury it!

☞ Wear old clothes—your good clothes might get wrecked.

BOYS RULE!

Camping
Instant Info

 One of the largest tents ever was made in 1952 and measured 28.1 metres by 14.6 metres.

 Scouts spend a lot of time camping. The Boy Scout movement was formed by Robert Baden-Powell in England.

 Campers learn to tell the best bedtime scary stories.

 Owls and other nocturnal creatures might disturb your sleep.

People go camping all over the world in tents of all shapes and sizes.

 The most common type of tent is a two-person tent.

BOYS RULE!
Think Tank

1 What should you do with your campfire before you go to sleep?

2 What is a teepee?

3 What do you do if the person who's sleeping in your tent snores?

4 Where do you go to the toilet when you are camping in a field?

5 What should you do with your rubbish when you leave the campsite?

6 What is the best food to eat when you go camping?

7 What do you do if a wild animal comes into your tent?

8 What do mosquitoes like to eat most of all?

Answers

1 Always put your campfire out … always.

2 A teepee is a tent Native Americans use.

3 If someone in your tent snores, put in earplugs or tell them to sleep outside.

4 You go to the toilet behind a tree when you are camping in a field.

5 Never leave your rubbish—always take it with you.

6 Baked beans are the best food to eat when you are camping.

7 If a wild animal comes into your tent, scream or pretend to be asleep … and hope that it goes way.

8 Mosquitoes like to eat your blood most of all.

How did you score?

- If you got all 8 answers right then you can pack your tent and go camping.

- If you got only 4 answers correct pitch your tent in the garden.

- If you got fewer than 4 answers correct you'd better stay home … inside!

Felice → ← Phil

Hi Guys!

We have loads of fun reading and want you to, too. We both believe that being a good reader is really important and so cool.

Try out our suggestions to help you have fun as you read.

At school, why don't you use "Camping Out" as a play and you and your friends can be the actors. Set the scene for your play. Use your imagination and pretend that you are at your favourite camping spot. It is just starting to get dark.

So ... have you decided who is going to be Josh and who is going to be Con? Now, with your friends, read and act out our story in front of the class.

We have a lot of fun when we go to schools and read our stories. After we finish the kids all clap really loudly. When you've finished your play your classmates will do the same. Just remember to look out of the window— there might be a talent scout from a television station watching you!

Reading at home is really important and a lot of fun as well.

Take our books home and get someone in your family to read them with you. Maybe they can take on a part in the story.

Remember, reading is a whole lot of fun.

So, as the frog in the local pond would say, Read-it!

And remember, Boys Rule!

BOYS RULE!
When We Were Kids

Felice   *Phil*

Felice "Did you ever worry about wild creatures when you camped as a kid?"

Phil "Yeah, I remember once I was attacked while I was asleep in my tent."

Felice "Really? That's terrible!"

Phil "These creatures were really hungry for my blood."

Felice "That's shocking. And you survived."

Phil "Yeah, but only just."

Felice "So what were these vicious creatures?"

Phil "Some people call them cannibals, but I call them mosquitoes!"

42

BOYS RULE!
What a Laugh!

Q What did the mosquito say the first time it saw a camel's hump?

A Did I do that?

43

BOYS RULE!

Read about the fun that boys have in these **BOYS RULE!** titles:

Gone Fishing

The Tree House

Golf Legend

Camping Out

Bike Daredevils

Water Rats

Skateboard Dudes

Tennis Ace

Basketball Buddies

Secret Agent Heroes

Wet World

Rock Star

and more ... !

44